To my grandmother, Dorothy Holabird   KH

To my grandsons, Nat and Will, with love   HC

PUFFIN BOOKS

Published by the Penguin Group
Penguin Books Ltd, 80 Strand, London WC2R 0RL, England
Penguin Putnam Inc., 375 Hudson Street, New York, New York 10014, USA
Penguin Books Australia Ltd, 250 Camberwell Road, Camberwell, Victoria 3124, Australia
Penguin Books Canada Ltd, 10 Alcorn Avenue, Toronto, Ontario, Canada M4V 3B2
Penguin Books India (P) Ltd, 11 Community Centre, Panchsheel Park, New Delhi – 110 017, India
Penguin Books (NZ) Ltd, Cnr Rosedale and Airborne Roads, Albany, Auckland, New Zealand
Penguin Books (South Africa) (Pty) Ltd, 24 Sturdee Avenue, Rosebank 2196, South Africa

Penguin Books Ltd, Registered Offices: 80 Strand, London WC2R 0RL, England

www.penguin.com

First published by Aurum Press Ltd 1985
Published by Viking 2001
5 7 9 10 8 6
Published in Puffin Books 2002
3 5 7 9 10 8 6 4

Manufactured in China by South China Printing Ltd. Co.

British Library Cataloguing in Publication Data
A CIP catalogue record for this book is available from the British Library

ISBN 0–670–91155–0 Hardback
ISBN 0–140–56865–4 Paperback

To find out more about Angelina, visit her web site at **www.angelinaballerina.com**

Angelina's Christmas

Story by **Katharine Holabird** Illustrations by **Helen Craig**

PUFFIN

Christmas was coming, and everyone at Angelina's school was working hard to prepare for the Christmas show. Angelina and the other children stayed after their lessons to rehearse and help decorate the hall.

When Angelina left school it was already dark outside. Large snowflakes were falling and Angelina was so excited that she danced along the pavement.

The cottages in the village looked warm and welcoming, with holly wreaths on the doors and Christmas lights shining in all the windows; but the very last cottage was cold and dark. Angelina peeped in the window and saw an old gentleman huddled by a tiny fire.

Angelina ran the rest of the way home and found her mother and little cousin Henry in the kitchen. She asked her mother about the man who lived all alone in the cottage.

"Oh, that's Mr Bell," her mother replied. "He used to be the village postman, but he's too old to work now."

Angelina decided that she wanted to make a Christmas surprise for Mr Bell, so Mrs Mouseling gave her some dough to make biscuits shaped like stars, bells, and trees.

Henry had a piece of dough too, and he made a nice big Father Christmas biscuit. "Look!" he said proudly. "I'm going to see Father Christmas tonight and give him this biscuit *myself*!"

"Father Christmas only comes very late at night after everyone has gone to bed," Angelina explained. "Why don't you leave your special biscuit out on a plate for him?"

Henry started to cry. "No!" he shouted. "I want to see Father Christmas!"

"Don't be such a crybaby, Henry," Angelina scolded, but Henry wouldn't stop crying.

The next afternoon Angelina and her mother
packed a basket with the biscuits, mince pies,
and fruit for Mr Bell. "Don't you want to help
Angelina take the presents to Mr Bell?" asked
Mrs Mouseling, but Henry only shook his head.

Then Angelina and her father went out to find a
Christmas tree for Mr Bell. Henry followed Angelina
and Mr Mouseling all the way to Mr Bell's cottage,
but he still wouldn't speak to them.

The old postman was amazed and delighted to see his visitors. He invited Angelina and her father inside, and then he noticed Henry standing alone in the snow. "Come in, my friend!" said Mr Bell with a smile, and he picked Henry up and brought him in near the fire.

Mr Bell's eyes were bright and twinkling. "Wait here a moment," he said, and disappeared up the stairs. Then he came down looking …

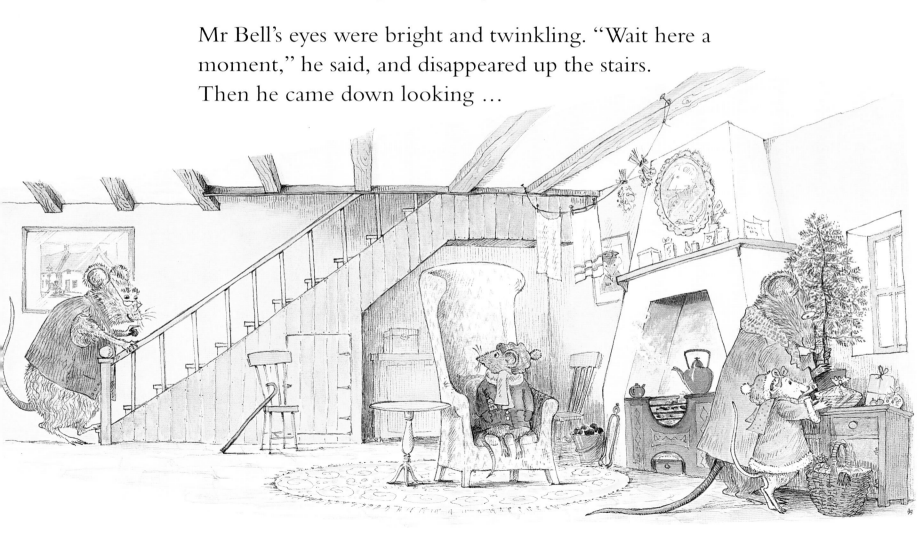

… just like FATHER CHRISTMAS!

"This is the red costume I wore once when Father Christmas needed someone to take his place at the village Christmas party," said Mr Bell with a chuckle, and he sat down with Henry on his knee. While Mr Mouseling made tea and Angelina decorated the tree, Henry listened to Mr Bell's stories.

"I used to go out on my bicycle, no matter what the weather was like, to deliver presents to all the children in the countryside. One year there was a terrible snowstorm and all the roads were covered with snow. I had to deliver the toys on a sledge, and if I hadn't glimpsed the village lights blinking in the distance, I would have been lost out in the storm." Henry listened with wide eyes.

When it was time to go, Henry reached into his pocket. "I made this," he said, "and I'd like to give it to you." Out of his pocket he took his big Father Christmas biscuit and gave it to Mr Bell.

"This is the best Christmas surprise I've had for many years," said Mr Bell, thanking Henry and Angelina for their presents. Angelina said she wished Mr Bell would come to her school show in his Father Christmas costume.

"That would be a pleasure," he said, smiling.

Mr Bell kept his promise: he came to the Christmas
show in his red costume and watched Angelina and

her friends dressed as sugar plum fairies
dancing the Nutcracker Suite.

Later all the children gathered round Mr Bell, and
Henry felt proud as Mr Bell handed out the Christmas
presents and entertained everyone with stories about
his adventures as a postman.

Mr Bell was never lonely at Christmas again, because every year he was invited to come to Angelina's school show dressed as Father Christmas.